DON'T BURN DOWN DOWN *the* BIRTHDAY CAKE

by joe wayman

ISBN 0-945799-00-4

Heartstone Press, 1988 Houston, Texas

Designed and Illustrated by Joseph Wayman

First published in the United States in 1988
by Wayman-Horn Associates

SPECIAL THANKS

Nancy L. Johnson---

My very special friend. Thank you for being so
persistent and stubborn. Thank you for pushing me beyond
myself and into these poems. Your heart has been my strength.

Billy Wayne Horn---

My special friend and colleague. Thank you for your
clear, objective eye and heart. You made me struggle a
little harder for the depth and meaning I was trying so
hard to find. Your honesty helped me speak more
clearly and fine-tuned my discipline.

DEDICATION

I dedicate this book
first to
Mom and Dad
The very best two parents
I have ever had.

I also dedicate these words
to sister Lynne and sister Sue.
They never could have happened
without growing up with
You.

a note from the author

I try to write the words
and nothing happens.
Then, in a most unexpected moment,
just after daybreak,
looking through the silent curtains
at the soft, new morning,
then,
when the quiet is part of me
and my heart beats
with the earth,
then,
the words begin...

They spatter out in all directions
like rain on pavement.
They run in rivers,
colliding, helter-skelter
into one another in a
jumbled, rapid-fire and uncontrollable surge of
conscious-unconscious, logical-illogical, disorganized
yet somehow directed and
purposeful
deluge.

Thoughts and feelings rush out as if they
needed to.
Chased by some unknown
devil as if they had to tell someone,
anyone.
As if they had a life of their own,
an independent need to be...

We move from mind and thought to page and print.
We breathe on our own. And for a few seconds
of intense
existence
we do not need the writer nor the pen.
We simply are. Hovering in space
between the creator
and the
page.
We have our own desperate and determined,
unrelenting need to explain something.

Life?
Struggle?
Pain?
Joy?
Hope?
Love?
Fear?

And then we fall upon the page
and our essence
becomes nothing more than waiting
until you pick us up,
give us life again
through your eyes.
And at that moment we move back from
page and print to mind and thought.
We live again in you.
Sometimes brief seconds of life.
Yet,
at other times you carry us around,
digest and muddle over us
and we gain an immortality
of
sorts.

We become a part of you
and in the years of your future
you nurture us
in quiet moments.

You look out at daybreak
through the silent
curtains,
at the soft, new morning
and you remember
with longing and love
the poem
you once
read.

Sincerely,
Joe Wayman.

FENCES

I wasn't good at kickball.
As a catcher I was bad.
The basketball eluded me.
As a runner it was sad.

But one thing I was good at,
Better than the rest.
When it came to climbing fences,
Clearly, I was best.

I'd hit a fence at sixty,
Grabbing madly for the top,
Throw one leg over, then the next,
Push away and drop!

Landing on the other side,
With a soft but solid plop,
I'd conquered one more fence,
And for the moment I could stop.

'Cause fences are like mountains,
At least to kids of eight or nine,
Just begging to be conquered,
Just waiting to be climbed.

Now grown-ups say that fences
Let you know where you should be.
Like rules we have to live by,
They keep things orderly.

But when I was a kid,
Somehow I didn't know.
So breaking all the rules,
Over fences I would go.

And now that I am all grown up,
It seems to me I find,
Some people building fences
Of a very different kind.

As long as some folks build them,
Build them high or build them wide,
I'll keep on climbing fences,
I need to know the other side.

And for every fence they build,
When all is done and said,
I think I'll try, for all my days,
To build a bridge instead.

GROWING UP

Only yesterday they say,
I was just a little kid.
Who couldn't reach the handle,
And who couldn't reach the lid.

My relatives who visit,
Always marvel at my speed,
Exclaiming that I'm sprouting up,
Just exactly like a weed.

And every time I turn around,
My head is farther from the ground.
The trousers that we bought last night,
Today don't seem to fit just right.

My zipper wouldn't yesterday,
My button popped at lunch,
My cuffs are at my elbows,
And I simply have a hunch.

I'm getting big, I'm growing up,
I'm always popping stitches.
And I guess that's what my father means,
When he says I'm too big for my britches.

Growing up is hard to do,
Parents wish you'd do it fast.
And then they moan a deep lament,
How childhood doesn't last.

GRANDMA-GREAT

Grandma-Great they call her,
And I agree it's true.
But I have two more grandmas,
And I think they're GREAT too!

A MOTHER'S TRIAL

Bundle up to go outside,
It's winter don't you know?
I always have to bundle up,
Or Mom won't let me go.

First the socks, a flannel shirt,
A sweater over that.
Earmuffs, gloves, galoshes too,
A fat and furry hat.

Corduroys tucked into boots,
Leggings over those,
A winter coat, five-hundred pounds,
A muffler for my nose.

And when the final scarf is wrapped,
And everything is zipped and snapped,
I look at Mom and softly say,
I have to pee before I play.

BLOW THE OTHER WAY

I get to stay in bed today,
I caught the common cold.
No homework and no chores today,
At least that's what I'm told.

I think I'll have a lot of fun,
Just staying here in bed.
I need a rest, but I'm perplexed,
Is this cold in my head?

Here's a hanky, keep it handy,
I do what I'm told,
But who can use a hanky,
When it's crusty and it's old?

I dribble and I run,
I cough and hack and wheeze,
No one can get near me,
'Cause they shower when I sneeze.

My eyes are red, my headache hurts,
My nose is bright, bright red.
My ears are clogged, my throat is sore,
I'm bored here in this bed.

The vaporizer fills the room,
With steam and fog and mist,
They smear my chest with greasy-goo,
I protest but they insist.

I gargle with some nasty stuff,
I doubt that it's a cure,
I thought I'd have a lot of fun,
But now I'm not so sure.

They tell me it will just take time,
Seven days at most.
Then this cold will go away,
And find another host.

So I'll keep sneezing, coughing too,
But I'll always hear them say,
Turn your head, cover-up,
and BLOW THE OTHER WAY!

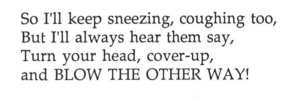

IF IT ISN'T ONE THING, IT'S ANOTHER

If it isn't one thing, it's another,
Something going wrong.
Just get one thing fixed,
And then another comes along.

Will I ever get it all worked out?
Will there ever be a time?
When everything is copacetic?
When everything is fine?

First my shoelace falls apart,
I have to tie it in a knot.
I get my sweater buttoned up,
But it's buttoned inside out.

Just when it's time to go,
My zipper seems to stick.
Fuss and fidget, pull and push,
I fix it double-quick.

Running to the bus,
I trip and rip my jeans.
I thought today would start out right,
But nothing's as it seems.

Forgot my homework, dropped my books,
Then sat down on a tack.
Billy hit me with his lunch,
I had to hit him back.

His big sister caught me,
Kicked me in the chin,
It's the same old story,
That's how my days begin.

Now I'm in trouble one more time,
I'm sitting in the hall.
I couldn't bring my homework,
So I'm writing on the wall.

And as I head for home,
Teacher sent a note.
I haven't read it yet,
But do you think I won't?

And I'll be deep in trouble,
Just one more time today.
But that's the way it always goes,
Is there any other way?

If it isn't one thing, it's another,
Something going wrong.
Just get one thing fixed,
And another comes along.

SCHOOL NURSE

The school nurse is ten feet tall,
With needles that will stick you to the wall.
You have to go if she should call,
You'll die of fear halfway down the hall.

Your knees will turn to jelly,
Your stomach turn to ice,
Your breath will come in tiny gasps,
As if your chest were in a vice.

When you reach her office door,
The smells will make you faint.
The lady just behind the desk,
Will say you have to wait.

The first kid who comes out of there,
His head wrapped up in white,
Tries a crooked, painful grin,
And you stand up stiff with fright.

All at once it's your turn next,
Go in and close the door.
You know that this must be the end,
Quote the raven "Nevermore!"

Kids who have to see the nurse,
Leaving class to go downstairs,
Simply seem to disappear,
And vanish in thin air.

So be careful and be on your guard,
If she calls you to her door.
Change your name, change your seat,
Or you'll be gone forevermore.

BEST OF FRIENDS

I have a bunch of best of friends,
I love each one the most.
And if I sound a bit too proud,
I don't mean it just to boast.

Some folks say that when you love,
There's only room for one.
But if you love and love just one,
You've only just begun.

Something magic happens,
When you let love in your heart.
Your heart just seems to grow a bit,
Larger now than at the start.

And when you think your heart is full,
With no more space to fill,
You'll find another best of friends,
And your heart gets bigger still.

So have a bunch of best of friends,
And love each one the most.
Go ahead and feel right proud,
Go ahead and boast!

FRIENDSHIPS

Sometimes some things happen,
You can't help it, they just do.
Like when you lose your closest friend,
And there's no one left but you.

One day everything is fine,
Your friend and you together.
Laughing, running, jumping, playing,
Life is sunny weather.

You tell each other secrets,
Run around the block.
Sleep out back in sleeping bags,
Stay up all night and talk.

You ride your bikes to school,
Rummy-dummy side by side.
Share your lunch, laugh a bunch,
Have a secret place to hide.

And when you have a dime,
Even if you're poor,
Half of it is for your friend,
That's what friends are for.

And then there comes a day,
Something's gone from your friend's eyes.
That friendship simply slipped away,
You think you want to cry.

You ride your bike to school alone,
Keep your secrets locked away.
Eat your lunch all by yourself,
Find a private place to play.

Friendships come, sometimes they go,
There's no one you can blame.
Happy in the starting, painful in the parting,
Just be glad that friendship came.

So wish your friend the best of luck,
You helped each other grow.
Be glad you shared a little time,
Now it's time for letting go.

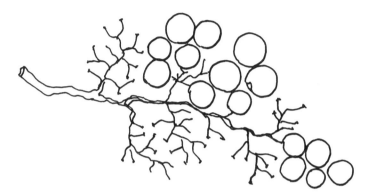

POCKETS

Pockets in your pants, pockets in your pants,
You have to have some pockets in your pants.
If your pockets were all gone, you couldn't take your stuff along,
You have to have some pockets in your pants.

Pockets are for things I need when I am getting bored.
Places where my very special treasures can be stored.
A place for all my marbles, some crackers and a rock,
A ball of string tied up in knots, a tiny ticking clock.

Paper clips, a ball of clay, a plastic ring, some sand.
The penny that I found today, a purple rubber band.
A wind-up bear without a key, a broken ballpoint pen,
Lint, some dust and lots of thread, odds and ends and then...

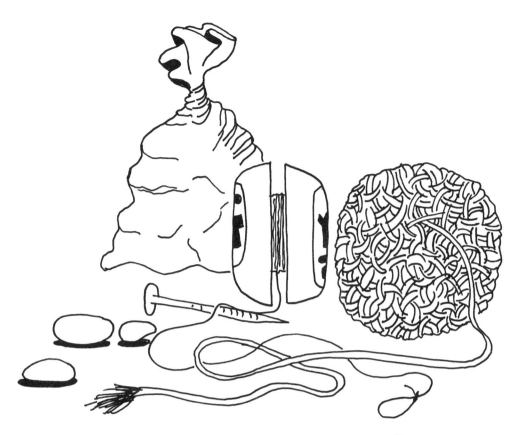

In this second pocket, I have some more great stuff.
There's lots of room, it's very large, I hope it's large enough.
A wrist watch with a broken dial, it's always just past lunch.
A bent and rusty nail file, some grapes, just half a bunch.

And over here I keep my cash, three nickels and a dime.
And then in this one under here some things I need to hide.
One last pocket, look and see, some pebbles in a sack.
Now I'm sure you'd like to see the stuff I keep in back!

Pockets in your pants, pockets in your pants,
You have to have some pockets in your pants.
If your pockets were all gone, you couldn't take your stuff along,
You have to have some pockets in your pants.

SCUFFLE, SCUFFLE

Scuffle, scuffle, feel the beat,
Of summer dust, of summer heat.
Scuffle, scuffle, love the sound,
Of summer feet on dusty ground.

Scuffle, scuffle, kick a stone,
Down dusty streets as dry as bone.
Scuffle, scuffle, where's the rub,
A little quicker in the tub.

Scuffle, scuffle, summer's done,
Gone the dust, gone the fun.
Scuffle, scuffle, autumn leaves,
The crumpled clothes of naked trees.

Scuffle, scuffle, don't be sad,
Winter slush is twice as bad.
Scuffle, scuffle, comes the Spring,
What sweet delight the mud can bring.

Scuffle, scuffle, whisper feet,
Every time they hit the street.
Scuffle, scuffle, all year round,
No wonder parents curse the ground.

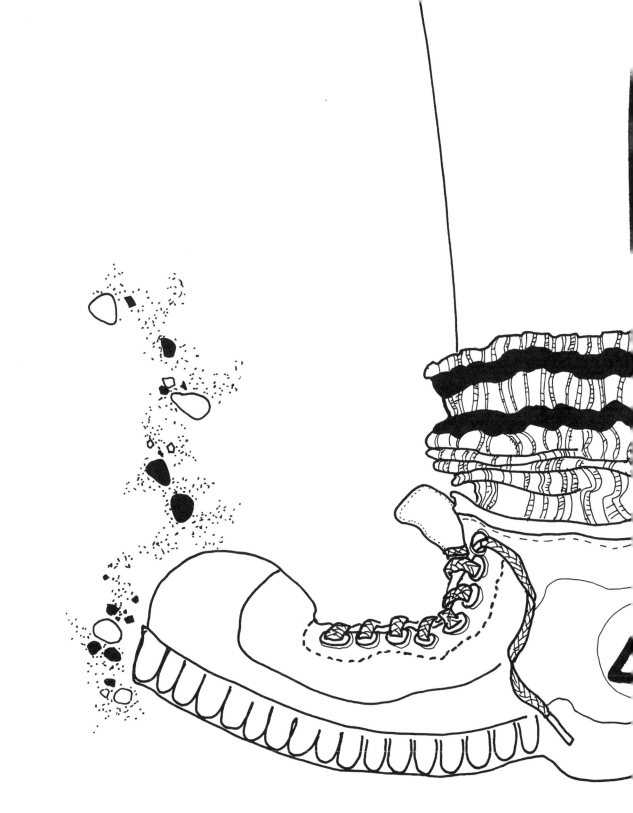

FASTER THAN A SPEEDING BULLET

When I got my first bike,
It had to be the best.
It had to be the biggest,
And the fastest in the West.

It had to have a basket,
And a carrier in the back,
Fenders on the wheels,
Chain guard, horn and rack.

So the morning after Christmas,
Beneath a frozen sky,
From the top of our big hill,
I jumped on and let-her-fly!

Past the Shefield house I zoomed,
The Bennett place flashed by.
A streak of kid at light speed,
To the neighbor's naked eye.

And as I reached about a thousand miles an hour,
I knew that I could make that big bike GO!
In that self same and solitary moment,
I knew that stopping was the part I didn't know!

PORCHES

Grandma seems to think
That porches are for sitting.
Sitting up on top of them
With time to do some knitting.

And that is partly true,
Porches are for sitting.
But sitting UNDER them I swear,
For kids, is much more fitting.

Grandmas sit and look about,
Watching neighbors come and go.
Nod and smile, wave hello,
Knit and pearl and throw.

Kids all sit right under them,
Watching spiders come and go.
Scream and hide and giggle,
In the crawl space down below.

While Grandmas rock on top,
With their coffee and their cake,
Kids below make sacred pacts
They promise not to break.

These two worlds are closely bound,
Yet forever far apart.
Held together by the
Knitting
And the
Porches
And
The
Heart.

All the world is not a stage,
Perhaps it's just a porch.

31

The sidewalk stretched out
like an airport runway
waiting for our
wheels.

MR. THOMAS   We clamped them on our shoes
with an iron key.

HATED   Then hung the key around
our neck on a piece
of butcher's

SKATES   string.

Our driveway
from the road
was mud
and
dirt.
Mr. Thomas' driveway was
blacktop from the
front sidewalk,
past the yards,
swooping by the front porches,
on between the houses,
pitching at a crazy angle,
down,
toward the back
yard,
rushing by the
gardens,
between
the garages
and
finally
into the
back
alley.

Our wheels roared.
They echoed off the
houses and
reverberated to the
heavens as our
747 minds took us
at the speed of light
down that
driveway.
Mr. Thomas hated skates,
at least until the year
he had to have a
hearing aid
and then
he didn't
yell at us
to quit
any
more.

KICK THE CAN

Kick the can!
Kick the can!
We played kick the can!

Underneath the street light,
We jumped and hid and ran.

Into the darkness, out of the light.
Into the darkness, into the night.

"Olly, Olly Oxford,
"Come in free!"
Yell it out!
You're out!
Lights out!

The can rattles
into the gutter.

Kids scatter behind
locked
doors.

Houses close their eyes.

Night lives outside
in
satin
silence.

Game's over.

TEDDY BEAR

I first saw him sitting there,
A great big fat and furry bear.
Bright and shiny button nose,
Yellow zippers, boots and bows.

I knew at once he had to be,
A Teddy Bear meant just for me.
I picked him up, he seemed to fit,
He snuggled 'neath my chin a bit.

That Teddy Bear came home with me,
And sometimes sits upon my knee.
I bump him sometimes on his head,
And thump him till he must be dead.

I snuggle him and huggle him.
He's always there through thick and thin.
My friend when I have messed up bad.
My friend when I am sad or glad.

When I fall and skin my knee.
He's always waiting there for me.
When I need a special friend,
He sits beside me till the end.

The world is filled with pain and care,
And when there's sorrow I must share,
I'll make it through 'cause he is there,
Teddy Bear, my Teddy Bear.

Especially for

Nancy L. Johnson

And when he's gone and lost his hair,
And when his fuzz is almost bare,
I'll love him then, yes, I'll still care,
Teddy Bear, my Teddy Bear.

BAGGAGE

ANYTHING CAN HAPPEN

Anything can happen in a place called "just imagine".
Shake the world and turn it all around.
Upside down and inside out, topside over under,
Find out what it's all about to wonder.

Remember you might never see,
That purple cow I speak of,
But in imagination you can find,
The things you dream of.

Birds can talk on telephones.
Grass can come up red.
Wind can really whisper,
And flowers sleep in bed.

Fish might fly and dogs meow.
Cats might eat bananas.
Anything can happen,
Even cows might wear pajamas.

Rain might fall up from the ground.
Elephants wear braces.
Puppy dogs might go to church,
Turtles win in races.

Jell-O might stop wiggling,
Hyenas might not laugh,
Anything can happen,
Even fish might take a bath.

Anything can happen in a place called "just imagine".
Shake the world and turn it all around.
Upside down and inside out, topside over under,
Find out what it's all about to wonder.

Remember you might never see,
That purple cow I speak of.
But in imagination you can find,
The things you dream of.

DON'T BURN DOWN THE BIRTHDAY CAKE

Happy birthday to you,
Happy birthday to you,
Happy birthday dear DRAGON,
Happy birthday to you.

Don't burn down the birthday cake,
Please for heaven's sake.
Don't burn down the birthday cake,
That's a promise dragons just can't make.

A dragon threw a party,
On his birthday just last May.
Everyone who came,
Thought it would be a lovely day.

But dragons never learned,
How to entertain too well,
The party was disastrous
The story I will tell.

The guests began to gather,
At the entrance to his den.
The jolly dragon by mistake,
Breathed some fire at them.

They jumped and turned as if to run,
In fear of being roasted,
But it was much too late,
So they came in quite well toasted.

First, he burned off all their hair.
They said they didn't care.
Then he served the ice cream up,
And melted every share.

It's just too much they all agreed,
But what else could go wrong?
So they finally decided,
They would stay and string along.

The dragon made a wish and
Blew the candles out.
Instead he fried the birthday cake,
His guests were left without.

With much chagrin, he would try,
To be a bit more careful,
And they believed he really would,
And felt a bit more cheerful.

Open all your presents now,
It's time to see inside.
Mr. Dragon turned around,
Forgetting that behind.....

His mighty tail squashed every gift,
The large ones and the small.
Not a single box was left,
To open, none at all.

The guests all got up in disgust,
"It's time to go," they sighed.
They saw the dragon much distressed,
He sat down and he cried.

"The den's a wreck," he moaned and groaned,
"I've spoiled everything."
"Besides burning down the birthday cake,
"I just can't sing!"

His friends decided there and then,
You really don't need cake.
And ice cream would melt anyway,
And gifts, for heaven's sake!

They didn't matter half as much,
As a dragon in a den,
Who always could and always would,
Try to be your friend.

43

A dragon is a pesky thing,
With wings and lots of scales,
With breath of fire to roast and toast,
A long ungainly tail.

But if you put up with his faults,
To his weaknesses be blind.
A dragon's just as true a friend,
As you will ever find.

Don't burn down the birthday cake,
Please for heaven's sake.
Don't burn down the birthday cake,
That's a promise DRAGONS just can't make.

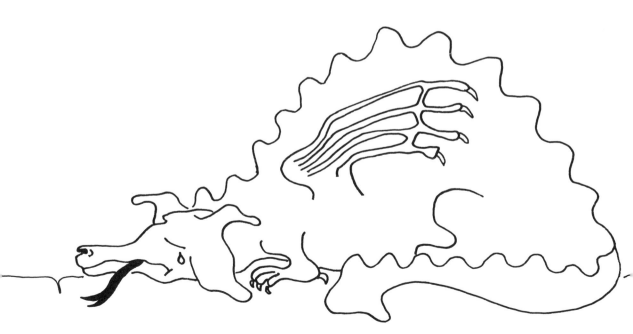

CAT

Cat,
you know where it's at.
Cat,
life's getting you so fat.
I don't care, I know you're there,
Cat.

Feline,
you're doing fine.
Feline,
you're doing so fine.
Sweet and low, moving slow,
Feline.

Tom,
what's gone wrong?
Old Tom,
you've been fighting so long.
Hurting life,
angry life,
Tom.

Kitty,
you're sitting pretty.
Kitty,
easy life in the city.
Day's for play,
play it away,
Kitty.

Cat,
you know where it's at.
Cat,
life's getting you so fat.
I don't care,
I know you're there.
Cat.

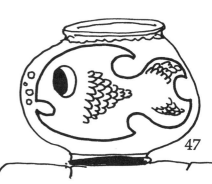

47

PEE WEE

I remember Pee Wee,
He was tiny when we met.
A German sheepdog puppy,
I never dreamed how big he'd get.

Pee Wee used to piddle,
In the middle of the floor.
Then he'd walk around in it,
And track it out the door.

Mother used to fuss and fume,
Rail at him and scold,
She called him piddle-paddler,
And he was only eight weeks old.

He never learned to heel,
He never learned to stay,
And when he dug the dahlias up,
We loved him anyway.

He wasn't good at guarding,
His tail gave him away,
Everybody was his friend,
He thought they came to play.

He never bit a living soul,
Although he licked a few to death,
He'd lick until you laughed so hard,
You couldn't catch your breath.

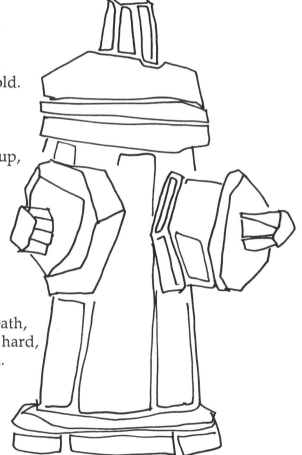

He never learned to growl,
And he never learned to bite.
He learned to love and show it all,
Instead of learning how to fight.

And when I think about him,
His total gift for giving,
I hope I learned a tiny bit,
About this thing called living.

SMORGASWORD

Tomatoes, potatoes,
Pumpkins and peas.
Rhubarb and parsley,
Watercress please.

Zucchini and eggplant,
Cabbage and kale.
Lettuce and okra,
Leeks without fail.

Crookneck, parsnips,
And broccoli tops.
Sirloin and T-bone,
Pot roast and chops.

Gooseberries, chokecherries,
Pie cherries too,
Strawberries, raspberries,
Mulberries blue.

There's sweet corn, cream corn,
Corn on the cob.
String beans, green beans,
And purple bean pods.

Home fries and french-fries,
Twice baked and mashed.
Broiled and boiled,
Patties and hashed.

There's scrambled, there's omelets,
And sunny-side up,
Soft-boiled, hard-boiled,
And poached in a cup.

There's white sauce, brown sauce,
Cheese sauce and chicken,
Custard and butterscotch,
Chocolate for lickin'.

Hollandaise, wine sauce,
And meat marinade,
Cream sauce and mushroom,
And sweet marmalade.

Cream us and stew us,
Fry us and bake.
Eat till you groan,
And then please pass the cake!

ABSURD

The ketchup, it was stubborn,
That's how it all began.
I should have known it then,
Before the gravy hit the fan.

The bottle slipped a little bit,
It landed in my plate,
I can't believe what happened next,
It must have been my fate.

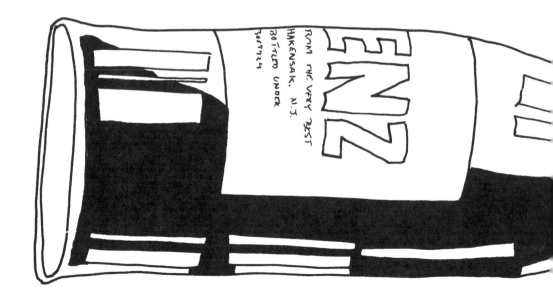

I dropped the Jell-O in the bowl,
It landed with a plop!
Mother sighed, Father yelled,
"Go and get the mop!"

I forgot to watch my elbow.
First I hit the salt.
Over went a glass of milk,
Was it really all my fault?

Mashed potatoes on my face,
Peas piled on my plate,
I tried to keep them off the floor,
I grabbed a bit too late.

Peas were rolling everywhere,
Mom was in a tizzy.
I tried to pick'em up too fast,
I guess I got too busy.

Chicken soup was suddenly,
Running off the table,
Noodles dropped off one by one,
With them came the ladle.

Noodles on linoleum,
What an awful mess.
Now they're down there mixed with peas,
I did it, I confess.

I jumped to grab the gravyboat,
It landed with a clatter,
"Good gravy!" cried my mother,
But by now it didn't matter.

The floor was getting deep,
The mess was getting bad.
Gravy, noodles, milk and peas,
My dad was getting mad.

Then, as quick as it had started,
It all came to a stop.
Mother started laughing,
And Dad began to mop!

I know I'm rather messy,
Clumsy is the word,
But when you're growing up,
Being perfect, that's ABSURD!

THE CLEANING MACHINE

Suzy Slop loves to mop.
The more she mops the more she slops.
The more she slops the more she mops.
We all wish that she would stop.

The more she cleans the more it seems,
The mess is much worse than before.
The more she scrubs, the more she rubs,
Seems there's more dirt on the floor.

Suds in the air and suds on the stair,
She scrubs with the suds with a splash.
Give her a broom, but get out of the room,
Or she'll sweep you away with the trash.

And Suzy must, she simply must dust.
She dusts everything night and day.
The walls and the floors, the halls and the doors,
Watch out or she'll dust you away.

Suzy it seems is a cleaning machine,
And her cleaning makes such a commotion.
She dusts and she scrubs as she slops and she mops,
As she cleans in perpetual motion!

GAG!

Spinach!
Gag!
Asparagus!
Gag!
Broccoli!
Gag!
Brussels Sprouts!
Gag!
Peas!
Gag!
Cauliflower!
Gag!
Zucchini!
Gag!
Lima Beans!
Gag!
Cabbage!
Gag!
Artichokes!
Gag!
Squash!
Gag!
Okra!
Gag!
Turnips!
Gag!
Parsnips!
Gag!
Celery!
Gag!
Sauerkraut!
Gag!
Liver!
Double Gag!

PERMISSION

When I ask Mom,
She says, "Go ask your dad."
So I ask him and I say,
"I already talked to Mom,
"She said it was O.K."

That way Mother gets the credit,
And Father has his say.
And as for me, as you can see,
That's how I get my way.

TAPPING

Quit tapping on the table with your fork!
Tap...tap...tap...
I said quit tapping!
Tap...tap...tap...
Quit it!
Tap...tap...tap...
You said with my fork!
Tap...tap...tap...
Well, stop tapping with your foot!
Tap...tap...tap...
Or with anything!
Tap...tap...tap...
Just quit tapping!

Shoot. I can't do anything!

SHARE AND SHARE ALIKE

They say you have to share,
And grown-ups all agree,
I'm supposed to share with you,
You're supposed to share with me.

So everything of mine is yours,
And all your stuff is mine.
I can't tell where it belongs,
Because we're sharing all the time.

Share your ice cream.
Share your lunch.
Share your candy,
Share your punch.

Share the bathroom,
Share the tub.
Share the soap,
And share the rub.

Share the blanket,
Share the bed,
Share the pillows,
For your head.

Share your racer,
Share your rocket.
Share the marbles,
In your pocket.

Share the window,
By the door.
Share the soldiers,
On the floor.

Share your time,
On Grandma's lap.
Share the time,
You take a nap.

Share your clothes.
Share your bike.
Learn to share,
And share alike!

Now everything I have I share,
Sharing, well, it's only fair.
And just to prove that this is true,
Here! I'll share my PEAS with you!

PERFECT

I am someone tried and true,
I'm sure you'd like to know me.
They tell me I'm a perfect child,
Grown-ups want to own me.

I'm honest as the day is long,
Just as sweet as pie.
Good as gold, right as rain,
The apple of your eye.

I'm just as quick as lightning,
Busy as a bee I am,
Pretty as a picture,
And as happy as a clam.

I'm quiet as a door mouse.
Sharp as any tack,
Bright as a new penny,
Wise as an owl in fact.

And then the other side of me,
As stubborn as a mule,
Mean as any junkyard dog,
Breaking every rule.

Angry as an old, wet hen,
Sly as any fox,
Crazy as a bedbug,
A face for stopping clocks!

As slippery as an eel,
Sneaky as a snake,
Mad as any hornet,
Nutty as a fruitcake.

Now you know both sides,
The sour and the sweet,
Which one of the two of me,
Would you like to meet?

DID TOO! DID NOT!

Did too!

Did too!

Did too!

Did too!

Did too!

Did too!

Did too!

Did too!

Did too!

Did too!

Did too!

Did too!

Did too!

Did too!

Did not!

Did not!

Did not!

Did not!

Did not!

Did not!

Did not!

Did not!

Did not!

Did not!

Did not!

Did not!

Did not!

Did not!

PLAY THE GAME

Hello and how are you?
How you doing and what's new?
Just great, I'm fine,
Nothing much and how about you?

O.K., pretty good.
I really can't complain.
See you later, you take care,
That's how you play the game.

Good morning and good evening,
Good day and then good-bye.
Good tidings and good going,
Good gracious and good try!

Next time someone says hello,
There's something you might try,
Instead of making small talk,
Tell the truth and not a lie.

Tell them you don't feel so hot,
Tell them where you ache,
Tell them you have troubles,
There's not much more that you can take.

Or tell them you're ecstatic,
That life is more than fine,
That everything is copacetic,
And you're having a great time.

My guess is they will wonder,
If you are just a little sick,
And begging of your pardon,
Take their leave and double-quick.

O.K., pretty good.
I really can't complain.
See you later, you take care,
That's how you play the game.

TIMID

I can move without a sound,
You think I scarcely touch the ground.
Stealthy as a midnight cat,
Silent as that pussycat.

Like a shadow on the wall,
You won't hear me move at all.
Hold my breath I'll slide right by,
Silent as a butterfly.

I am the child you cannot see,
You're always overlooking me.
I'm living in a silent world,
In loneliness my life is curled.

I ask you stop, your heart will find.
A child is here, you are not blind.
Reach out and touch my soul awake.
Know the difference you can make.

For I can move without a sound,
You think I scarcely touch the ground.
Hold your breath, I'll slide right by,
Silent as a butterfly.

NOTHING IS AN EASY THING TO DO

Nothing is an easy thing to do,
All alone or with a friend or two.
Doing nothing is something I like to do.
And once in a while doing nothing is good for you.

You can do nothing sitting in a tree,
Or climbing to the top where you can see.
You can do nothing lying on your back,
Smiling at the sky while the sky smiles back.

Doing nothing with a friend once in a while,
Is doing something that will give your face a smile.
Try doing nothing with a friend and you will know,
It gives you time to watch your friendship grow.

Some people think that you should always be,
Doing something, as busy as a bee.
But take the time now and then and do,
NOTHING, it will help to see you through.

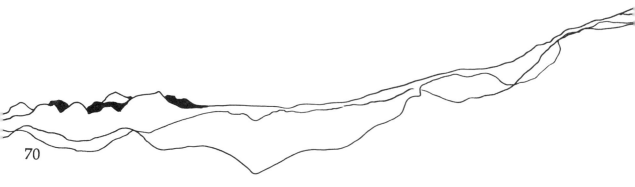

PLAYING POSSUM

I remember late night rides
from Grandma's house to home.
The rain had left the
streets glittering in
the late
night
neon.

Empty. The streets were.
And I watched from the back seat
as we passed over the viaduct
on the west side of town,
purred up Fourth South
past Main Street,
and hummed toward the
big
hill
that led up to
our
house.

When we started up the
hill,
I always used to fall
asleep.
That was so, when I
heard the gravel crunch
underneath the
wheels in our
driveway,
and Mom would say,
"Home again, home again,"
Then,
Dad would carry me
inside to my
bed,
thinking I was sound
asleep.

I loved to be carried
to
bed
at midnight
when
we got home
from
Grandma's.

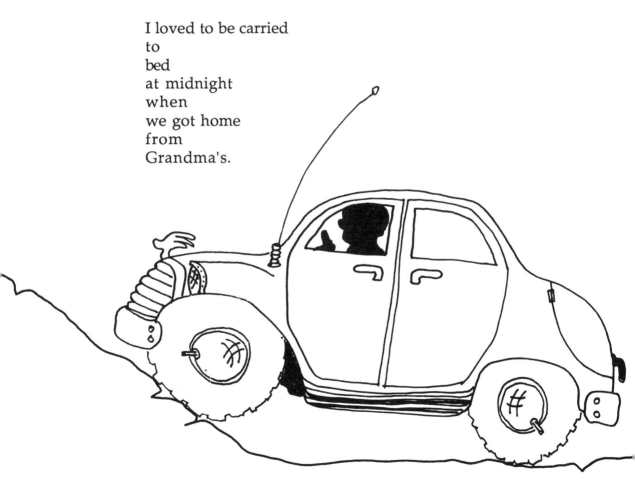

LIVING

Grandma Anderson
never died you know.
Even when they came
and took her
in that big
white
ambulance.

She didn't die.

I know she didn't.

Want to know how I know?

Because,
to this very day,
everytime I take a bite
of crusty homemade bread,
I can see her pounding out
the dough,
powdered white from
head to toe,
whistling backward
through her teeth
and perpetually
adjusting her
hearing aid.

I can feel the heat of that kitchen,
stumble over pieces of curled up linoleum,
and watch as fat, inflated loaves
of hot bread come out of the
oven and thump down
on the table
upside down
to
cool.

I can hear that funny
knife saw through that loaf and I can see
the butter melt into
its middle and I
can taste it on my tongue
as I bang out
the old screen door
at the side
of
that little house
at the end
of
Learned
avenue.

That's how I know.

WHITTLING

Tiny chips of wood
would spin away
across the yard
as Grandpa
whittled sticks with a
stainless steel
pocket-
knife.

He never made anything.
He just whittled
until the stick
was
gone.

He whistled
as he
whittled.

The world seemed so
safe
when I watched
Grandpa whittle sticks
away into nothing,
after dinner,
out back,
under the old
apple
tree.

I always wondered
why
he never made
anything.

But perhaps he did.

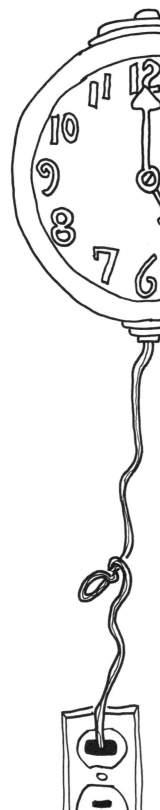

FIVE O'CLOCK

Dad came home each night at five,
Exactly on the nose.
Not ten-to-five or five-o-nine,
But FIVE and I suppose...

Mother found some comfort there,
Because she could always know,
We'd all be back together,
When our dad walked through that door.

Now we're grown, the years have flown,
We're living separate lives.
But the memory and the love remains,
And I always eat at five.

GREAT UNCLE WILL

Uncle Will was
already parchment
when I met him at the age
of
six.

Old, torn, tough.
Wrinkled,
folded, spindled
and
over the years
relentlessly
mutilated.

Craggy, baggy, wheezy.
Hacking in his handkerchief,
with beady eyes
like steel blue
bullets. His voice
an old victrola record
slowly
winding
down.

He gave me quarters
and chomping his
barren gums at me,
told me to bring him the
glass with his
teeth from beside
his
cot.

Covered up in coveralls.
His blue chambray shirt
buttoned to
his Adam's apple
and his shoes stuffed
with newspaper
to keep the
water
out.

His trailer stood by a big apple tree
and had
no lights,
no heat,
no water.

He must have been
somewhere around
ninety years old
when he died
in the fire.

That fire burned
Uncle Will's trailer
to the ground
and the old
apple tree
along
with
it.

Dad said his
mattress had been
stuffed with money.

Dad said
he had bank accounts
all over town.

Dad said
he must have been
worth
at least
a
million
dollars.

No one knows exactly.

80

WAITING

I really tried to wait,
Up, that is, for you.
But when it got so late,
There was nothing I could do.

My glasses sort of slowly slipped,
Down off of my nose,
My book fell from my hand,
And my eyes just softly closed.

I slipped into a gentle dream,
That you had just come home,
I told you how I'd missed you,
When I was here alone.

And when I wake up later,
The covers tucked beneath my chin,
My book and glasses put away,
I'll know that you looked in.

I'll know you said you love me,
I'll know you said good night.
I'll know I'll see your morning smile,
When the darkness turns to light.

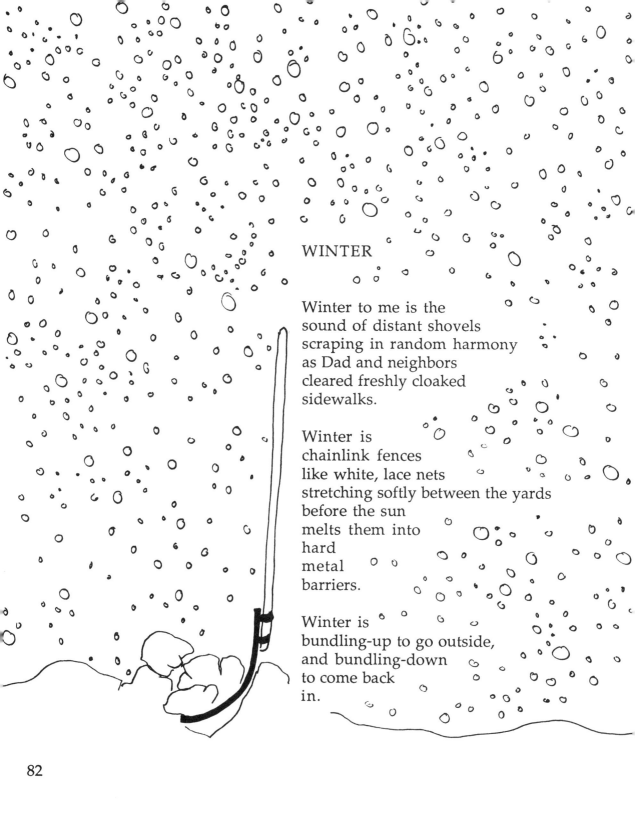

WINTER

Winter to me is the
sound of distant shovels
scraping in random harmony
as Dad and neighbors
cleared freshly cloaked
sidewalks.

Winter is
chainlink fences
like white, lace nets
stretching softly between the yards
before the sun
melts them into
hard
metal
barriers.

Winter is
bundling-up to go outside,
and bundling-down
to come back
in.

Winter to me is
angels on their back,
fox and chicken trails
in the front yard,
snow down my collar,
and numbness in my nose,
and in my fingers,
and mostly in my
toes.

Winter is clinkers
from the old, coal furnace
in the basement,
glowing hotly in the
clutches of those
monstrous tongs
as Dad removed them
each evening
at
bedtime.

And winter to me is
Grandpa and Grandma
ringing the
Christmas morning doorbell
long before Mom and Dad
were even out
of
bed.

Winter to me is
one of the
warmest seasons
of
my
heart.

SOMETIMES I FEEL...

Sometimes I feel scarlet
like a rose
in rampant,
cascading,
color.
Harmonies of laughter
and
vivid
giggles.

Sometimes I feel like mauve and taupe.
Like sun-drenched curtains,
too long in summer sun.
In shades like
almost
forgotten,
memories.

Sometimes I feel
lollipop-purple, popsicle-pink,
tickled into polka dots
of hilarious
wonder.

Sometimes I feel like
stripes going zigzag
across a broken, concrete floor,
jagged, in gray fragments of
lost hope.

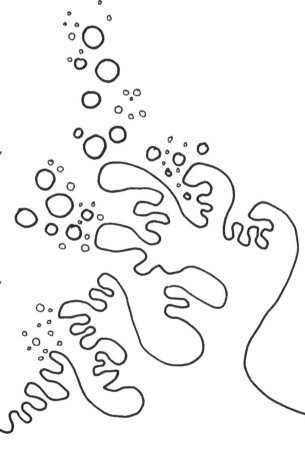

Sometimes I feel hot inside
like night-neon lights
blinking
in ragged, ice-blue patterns
of
remembered
pain.

Sometimes I feel
sibilant
like paisley
in turquoise,
aquamarine and
orange flashes
of
anger.

And sometimes I feel
multicolored,
technicolored,
reflected and
refracted,
like a
searchlight
in
time.

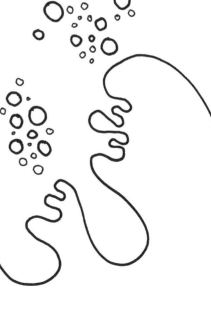

WHEN WHITE IS BLACK
AND
BLACK IS WHITE

Turn the bathtub upside down,
Do summersaults all over town.
Walk a windrow, paint a cake,
Giggle, jiggle, heaven's sake.

Watch me on the telephone,
Give your friendly bank a loan.
Send a bug a telegram,
Be as happy as a clam.

Dance on tiptoe, hug-a-bug,
Swing a beetle, chug-a-lug.
Freeze your nose in red hot June.
Toast your toes in winter's gloom.

Question every answer, yes.
Answer every question, guess.
When you are you will not be.
When you go, you stop you see.

When up is down and down is up,
It's much too full your empty cup.
When white is black and black is white,
You've won the war but lost the fight.

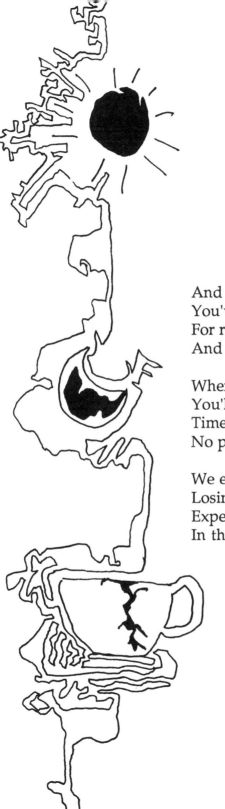

And when you really think you see,
You've just gone blind so let it be.
For right is wrong and bad is good.
And what you can't you really should.

When all of this is said and done,
You'll wonder if you had the fun.
Time stood still yet quickly fled.
No place to go yet still it led.

We end up at the starting place,
Losing hope yet full of grace.
Expecting judgment but instead,
In the silence, truth is said.

THE LAST TIME

There had to be a last time
I played hide-and-seek,
or
cowboys and indians.

There had to be a last time
the mailman brought me
a secret code ring.

Or a last time
I climbed our
big sycamore tree,
or
ran down our alley
in a
red Superman
cape.

There had to be a last time
I
hid under my bed,
or yelled,
"Can Paul come out to play?"
Or lay on my stomach
in the
fresh
cut
grass
and ate
stems.

Or the last time
my mother tended
my wounded knees.

And there had to be a last time
I ate
Campbell's tomato soup.
at the table
in the breakfast nook
in the house
where I
grew
up.

And there had to be a last time
I sat on our concrete
front porch
at the end of summer
and waited for the
winter.

I have done
so many things
for the
very
last
time.

INDEX

HEARTSTONE PRESS
P.O. Box 890686
Houston, TX 77289-0686

ISBN 0-945799-00-4